This book belongs to

Nicola   Patrica
Hunter. Thornton

Aged 11

STORIES FOR THE YOUNG READER

THE

Mouse's House

AND OTHER STORIES

STORIES FOR THE YOUNG READER

THE
Mouse's House
AND OTHER STORIES

p

This is a Parragon Book
This edition published in 2002

Parragon
Queen Street House
4 Queen Street
Bath BA1 1HE, UK

Copyright © Parragon 2000

ISBN 0-75258-422-7

Designed by Mik Martin

Printed in Italy

These stories have been previously
published by Parragon in the
Bumper Bedtime Series

CONTENTS

The Mouse's House

NOW THERE are those who enjoy keeping their things clean and tidy and there are those who don't. You can tell as soon as you step inside someone's front door which kind of home you are visiting. Of course, it is nice not to have to move piles of books and papers before you sit in a chair. And no one wants to find their plate covered in a thick layer of dust, but some people are *so* clean and tidy that it's no fun at all to pay them a visit. The Mouse was like that, as you will see.

The Mouse lived in a very cosy little tree-trunk house in the middle of Mendlesham Wood. She probably had been given a proper name when she was a baby, but everyone just called her "Mouse".

Mouse had always been proud of her home, and she had never been untidy. She liked everything to look just right, so that none of the other animals in Mendlesham wood could point their paws at her and say, "Have you *seen* the cobwebs in *her* house?"

But to begin with, Mouse was no more worried about dirt and dust than any moderately houseproud animal in the wood. The change was very gradual. For a long time, she swept her front steps once a day. Then you might sometimes see her,

especially in autumn, giving them a little extra sweep in the afternoon. By the time of this story, she was out on those steps half a dozen times a day.

"It's these horrible old leaves," she would say, if a friend protested that she was working too hard.

"But Mouse, you live in a *tree!*" the friend would say. "Of course there will be leaves."

"Not on my steps there won't!" replied Mouse stoutly, picking up her broom again.

Well, Mouse became as particular about the inside of her house as she was about her front steps. She was constantly dusting and sweeping and washing and wiping. She was a great plumper-up of cushions, too, and she had a hatred of spiders and their webs that would have been funny if it hadn't been rather worrying too.

"Out of my way," Mouse would say to a guest who had come to tea. "I saw one of those pesky little animals run under your chair. I can't rest until I've found him. The very thought of those eight muddy feet running over my floorboards makes me shiver and shake. Watch out! Don't spill your tea!"

It soon became something of a lottery to visit Mouse. You might have a perfectly lovely time, but on her worst days, Mouse was not a good hostess.

"Excuse me, but *did* you wipe your feet as you came in?" she would ask, peering suspiciously at your shoes. "Perhaps you wouldn't mind doing it again."

Then, after you had dutifully wiped them up and down several times on the doormat, Mouse would make a big point of shaking the mat itself outside the door. Of course, that might mean that she felt the step needed sweeping as well. So you see what I mean, conversation at Mouse's tea parties was often a little strained.

Gradually, the animals in

Mendlesham Wood became quite worried about Mouse.

"It isn't healthy to be so finicky," said the owl, whose own home was really none too clean. "Mouse is making herself ill worrying about things that don't matter at all. Why, when I visited her the other day, she told me I couldn't sit in the chairs because I'd flatten the cushions. I mean, what are chairs *for*? That's what I'd like to know."

"It was the same when I called to collect her grocery money," said the rabbit who lived under the old oak tree. "She wouldn't let me knock at the front door in case my paws were dirty. She was peering out of the window, waiting for me, so that she could catch me before I touched it!"

"That's dreadful," said the hedgehog. "Doesn't she know that a little bit of dirt is *good* for you. That's what I always tell my little ones."

Some of the others coughed and looked away. They knew very

well that the hedgehog and her little ones were never invited to Mouse's house because it was well known by everyone that they had *fleas*. Mouse hated fleas almost as much as she hated spiders. Just because they hopped instead of scurrying, it didn't mean that their feet were clean. Very few tiny creatures were welcome in Mouse's home, although she did have a soft spot for moths, for some reason.

"Someone should talk to her," said the owl. "A close friend, I mean," he went on hurriedly, "not someone like me who is really only an acquaintance."

"The sad thing is that she really

doesn't *have* any close friends any more," said the squirrel. "It is so uncomfortable to visit her now that nobody wants to do it. And it's hard to be close friends with an animal you hardly ever see. I can't remember the last time I visited Mouse's house, in fact. I miss having her as a friend."

"I think you're right," said the woodpecker. "I haven't seen her since I made that little attic window at the back for her a few years ago. She complained about the sawdust then, but she was nothing like so fussy as she is now. I don't think she could bear anyone to touch her house in any way."

The animals were well
meaning, but they couldn't really
think of any way to help Mouse. In

the end, it was a complete stranger who made a difference.

That winter was particularly cold. Even the trees shuddered as a howling, icy wind whistled around their roots and branches, frosting their twigs and chilling every little creature who lived nearby. All the animals huddled in their homes, doing the best they could to keep warm.

Mouse had a snugger home than most, especially as she always made sure that her window frames were free from draughts and her strong, tree-trunk walls were free from cracks.

But Mouse didn't like the way

that frost made her windows look dirty, and snow had a habit of dropping from the branches above and falling with an alarming *plop!* on to her steps.

It was on a particularly cold and blustery night that Mouse had an unexpected visitor. She was sitting in front of her fire, sipping a cup of apple tea, when she heard a little squeal outside and then a hammering at her door. Mouse tried to ignore it at first, but then the dreadful thought occurred to her that someone might actually be damaging her home. She pulled her shawl around her shoulders and opened the door.

Outside was a truly pitiful sight. A little mouse, no bigger than Mouse herself, was shivering on the doorstep.

"Please," he said, "could I come in to warm myself for a moment? I won't trouble you for long."

Mouse hesitated for just a second. She thought with horror of the mouse's wet little paws scampering across her sitting room. She shuddered at the thought of his cold, wet little body sitting on one of her chairs. She could imagine the way that he would shake his whiskers all over her carefully polished table. But Mouse could not bear to see another creature suffer, so she stood back from the door.

"Do come in," she said. "Er … the door mat is just here."

"Thank you so much," shivered the stranger mouse, as he stood in the middle of Mouse's sitting room. "I don't think I could have lasted much longer out there. It's no night for a mouse to be out."

"No, indeed," agreed Mouse. "Er … can I take your … er … coat?" She didn't really think that was the right word for the ragged, shapeless garment that the mouse held tightly around himself. But the mouse seemed to know what she meant and handed her the thin, wet cloth.

"I've been travelling for a long time," he said. "I'm on my way to see someone very special, but winter has been harder than I ever thought it would be. I should probably have put off my journey until the spring, but I was so eager to meet this person that I couldn't wait."

Mouse handed the stranger a towel to dry his whiskers before he shook them any more, but the visitor didn't seem to understand and wrapped the towel around his shoulders instead.

"Thank you again," he said. "I should introduce myself. My name is George."

The name sounded vaguely

familiar to Mouse, but she couldn't think why.

"My name is Mouse," she said. "It sounds strange, I know, but I think it's what I've always been called. I can't remember when I was a baby."

George nodded and sat down in the chair. Thankfully the towel was between him and the upholstery. Goodness knew when he had last taken a bath.

The newcomer was still shivering, so Mouse hurried to her neat little kitchen and made up a tray of hot soup, bread and juniper biscuits.

"I wasn't expecting visitors,"

she said, apologising for the makeshift supper. And all of a sudden she wondered why that was. There had been a time when her friends visited her every day, but she couldn't remember now the last time that anyone had dropped in.

George didn't find the supper disappointing at all. He was already finishing the soup and stuffing a rather large piece of bread into his mouth.

"This is wonderful," he said, between chews. "I haven't had anything to eat since the day before yesterday."

Mouse was horrified to hear

this. In fact, she was so concerned
that she didn't notice until it was too
late that George had put his hot
soup bowl down on her polished
table. She snatched it up with a cry.
Sure enough, there was a white ring
where the bowl had stood.

"Ooops, sorry," said George.

Mouse knew that she could not
possibly send her visitor out into the
blizzard again tonight. She hurried
upstairs and made sure that the
sheets on the spare-room bed were
aired. She slipped a hot water bottle
into the bed and ran back
downstairs again to try to stop
George doing any more damage to
her furniture. She was too late.

"I am ever so sorry," said George. "I don't know how it happened. One minute I was rocking myself gently in your chair and the next minute the leg fell off. It must have been a little loose, I think."

"Rocking?" said Mouse faintly. She looked up at the wall, and sure enough she could see the mark where the chair had been bumped over and over again. This mouse would bring her home down about her ears if he carried on at this rate!

Nevertheless, Mouse clenched her paws and asked George if he would like a bath before bed.

"That would be bliss," said

George. "I haven't had a bath since…"

"Yes, yes, that's all right," said Mouse hurriedly. She really didn't feel she could cope with the news George had been about to give her.

Five minutes later, Mouse, doing her best to tidy up downstairs, heard George singing at the top of his voice. It was a very silly song, and he wasn't remotely in tune, but still she caught herself smiling. It was such a long time since she had heard anyone really enjoying themselves in her house.

But Mouse's smile was not in place for long. She began to wonder what state the bathroom would be in when George had finished, and just then … *splosh!* … a drop of water bounced off her nose.

Mouse looked up in horror. There was no doubt about it, water was dripping through her beautiful ceiling and on to her sofa below.

Mouse hurried up the stairs and banged furiously on the bathroom door.

"W-w-w-what?" came a voice, after a moment. "Oh no! Oh, I am sorry. I dozed off for a moment and left the taps running. There's not much water on the floor though. Honestly, there isn't."

"That's because it's on the floor downstairs," muttered Mouse to herself, but she felt sorry for the little mouse who was so tired he had almost drowned himself.

A moment later, George appeared at the bathroom door, wearing a pair of Mouse's late father's pyjamas. He looked clean and scrubbed, but his eyelids were drooping, and he had one paw on the door frame to support himself as he said goodnight to his hostess.

"Goodnight," said Mouse. "I hope you sleep well."

It took Mouse another three hours to finish clearing up the sitting room *and* the bathroom, but then her standards were very high. She was exhausted herself when she finally tottered up the stairs to bed. And that is why she fell asleep the moment her head touched the pillow and didn't wake up at the crack of dawn as usual in the morning.

In fact, Mouse woke up feeling rather happy with the world. It took a few seconds for her to realise that this was because the smell of a fried breakfast and freshly brewed acorn coffee was wafting up the stairs.

Mouse sat up in bed. Someone was in her kitchen! Then the events of the night before came flooding back. Oh no! *George* was in her kitchen, and what was more, he was *cooking*!

Mouse flew out of bed and into her dressing gown. Her little feet hardly touched the stairs as she rushed towards the kitchen. One glimpse was enough to tell her that it was even worse than she had feared. There was George, his whiskers singed, flapping a tea towel at a flaming pan, while water running into the sink overflowed on to the floor. A second glimpse showed her two broken cups and a fish slice bent in two. And surely that wasn't … oh no, it couldn't be … that wasn't a *pancake* stuck to the ceiling? Mouse had to sit down in a hurry, and the floor was the nearest place.

"Oh, there you are," called George cheerfully. "I was just making you a little breakfast to thank you for being so kind. If you just wait there while I deal with this little fire, it will be ready for you in just a minute."

Mouse put her head in her hands. George was going to have to go, and he was going to have to go *soon*. She felt that every second that George spent in her house was another opportunity for disaster to strike.

But just at that moment, the visitor pushed a plate of pancakes and syrup under her nose. Much to Mouse's surprise, it smelt *delicious*! With all the excitement the night before, she remembered, she hadn't had any supper herself. Now she was too hungry to do anything other than pick up a spoon and start eating. And the pancakes tasted as delicious as they looked. How extraordinary!

As she munched her way through the pancakes, Mouse became aware that her visitor was talking.

"… so that's why I felt I just had to come and see her," he was saying. "I've heard so many stories about how kind she is to everyone, and how animals flock to see her when they are in trouble. Aunt Petunia sounds such a wonderful person. I don't suppose you know her, do you? She lives somewhere around here. In fact, I'm sure you two must be friends, for you are just as kind as she is. *Do* you know her, Mouse?"

Mouse had the strangest feeling in her tail and whiskers. Petunia! That was a name she hadn't heard for so long. For the first time in years, Mouse knew what her real name was. No wonder George had looked and sounded familiar. He was her own sister Salvia's son.

If Mouse hadn't been sitting down already, she would have done so now. Instead, she asked George if she could have some of his acorn coffee.

Huddled in her dressing gown, Mouse sipped the excellent coffee and thought hard. There *had* been a time when she cared more for others than for herself. What had happened? Mouse looked around her

home. In recent years, she had cared more for cleaning and tidying than for anything that was really important. Mouse felt ashamed. How could she confess who she was to this eager young mouse, when the evidence was all too plain that she only ever thought about her perfect home.

Then Mouse began to laugh. The evidence wasn't plain at all! Her kitchen was in ruins. The sitting room ceiling was soggy. There were marks on the walls and furniture, and she hadn't even looked to see what George had done to the spare room.

Mouse looked again at her

nephew. He was certainly a wonderful cook. He just needed a little guidance about safety and damage control. Mouse felt warmed by the idea that George might have to stay for a few weeks, months or even years, so that she could help him.

For the first time in ages, Mouse felt really happy, and that made her laugh too, especially as the flood on the floor was now creeping up her dressing gown.

"George," she smiled, "there's quite a lot I need to tell you…"

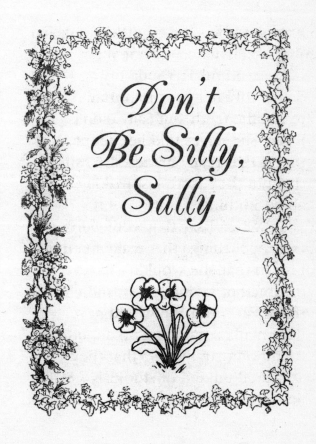

THERE WAS ONCE a little girl called Sally who was not very truthful. Her mummy and daddy told her how important it was to tell the truth, but Sally didn't listen. She never told lies about things that really mattered, so she thought they were just making a fuss about nothing.

When I say that Sally didn't tell lies about things that really mattered, I mean that she wouldn't have dreamed of saying she was ill when she wasn't. And she would never have made something up about a friend or a stranger so that they appeared unkind or stupid. No, Sally's lies were about silly things. In fact, when she was a baby, her parents thought she simply had a vivid imagination, and they liked her little stories. But now that she was older, it didn't seem so funny any more.

Let me tell you the kind of thing that Sally would say.

"I've only got one sock on," she would announce at breakfast, "because I gave the other one to an elf this morning."

"Don't be silly, Sally," her mother would say. "Go and find your other sock and put it on."

"I can't eat my breakfast," the little girl would go on, "because a rabbit came in the night and borrowed my teeth!"

"Don't be silly, Sally," her father would say. "Eat up like a good girl."

Then it would be time for Sally to go to nursery.

"I don't want to wear my red coat," she would wail. "It's not a red day today. It's a blue day."

"Don't be silly, Sally!"

"There are creepy-crawly things in my boots! I can't put them on."

"Don't be silly, Sally!"

And so it went on. All day long, Sally made up stories about everything she did or saw.

If Sally saw some flowers growing by the path on her way to nursery, she would say, "I know the

fairy who planted those. Her name is Annabel."

Sally's mummy and daddy hoped that their daughter was just going through a phase that would soon pass.

"She's a very imaginative little girl," said Sally's teacher. "It would be a shame to bring her down to earth too much."

"Just a little bit would be nice," said Sally's mummy. "I never know whether to believe her or not when she says something out of the ordinary."

Of course, as time went on, everyone believed Sally less and less. They got so used to her stories and inventions that they hardly listened to what she said. So when Sally came running in from the garden one day with important news, her mummy didn't pay too much attention.

"There's buzzing in the garage," cried Sally.

"Don't be silly, Sally," said her mother, automatically.

Sally went outside to play for a while. But after half an hour, she came running back inside.

"They're buzzing in and out," she said. "Like this." And she did a little dance in the middle of the sitting room.

"Don't be silly, Sally," said her

mother. "No one is dancing in our garden."

"Not in the garden," said Sally. "In the garage."

"Don't be silly, Sally. The only things in the garage are the car and the bookshelves that your father started before you were born and still hasn't finished," said Mummy.

So Sally went out to look again. When she came back, she was

holding something tightly in her striped mittens.

"Look," she said. "I caught one of the buzzy things."

"Don't be silly, Sally. There's nothing in your hands at all."

"Yes, there is," retorted Sally, and she opened her arms wide.

Sally's mummy carried on with her work, but a second or two later she quite distinctly heard a buzzing sound. It was a bee.

Then Mummy shut the doors and windows and called Daddy down from his workroom.

"There's a swarm of bees in our garage," she said. "Sally discovered them."

Daddy looked doubtful for a moment, but Mummy and Sally spoke together.

"No," they said, "it's *true*!"

Some men came to take away the bees before they stung anyone.

Mummy and Daddy listen a little more carefully to what Sally says these days. Perhaps that's why Sally doesn't make things up quite so often — except when she doesn't want to wear blue socks, of course. Then those naughty elves *will* come and steal them!

The Busy Baker

ONCE UPON A TIME, there was a very busy baker. He was busy because his bread and cakes and biscuits were the most delicious for miles around. If a person tasted just one of them, he or she would never want to eat anything made by another baker again.

The baker made bread that smelled heavenly and tasted so good that some people ate it just by itself without cheese or jam or honey.

The baker made cakes that melted in your mouth and made you wish you could eat them for breakfast, lunch *and* supper.

The baker made biscuits that were the crispest and crumbliest you have ever tasted. Many an important person in the town walked around with telltale crumbs on his waistcoat!

But it wasn't only because his baking was popular that the baker was so busy. The fact was that he was never satisfied with the wonderful things he made. He always had to be trying something to improve them, or working hard to invent a recipe that had never been made before.

So the baker worked night and day. His chimney could be seen smoking at midnight, and he was up again to make bread for the morning by three o'clock.

Of course, it is much easier to work hard at something you like than it is to put a lot of effort into a job you hate. But the baker was only human, and no one can go without sleep or rest or holidays for ever. It was inevitable that sooner or later, the baker would make a mistake.

This is how it happened. One day in early summer, a lady who lived very near the baker took her little niece into the bakery to choose a cake for her tea. The little girl's mummy was rather ill, which was why Anna-Maria was staying with her aunty. It was also why her aunty was trying to be specially nice to the little girl, although, to be honest, that was not always easy. Perhaps it was because she was worried about her mummy, but Anna-Maria was often a very difficult child.

As they stood looking at the wonderful selection of cakes and biscuits, Mrs Biddle (for that was the aunt's name) urged her niece to make her choice.

"I know they *all* look delicious," she said, "but you must choose just one of them. We can always come back tomorrow so that you can try something else."

But Anna-Maria looked at the lovely cakes and scowled.

"I can't see anything I want," she said.

"But darling," cried Mrs Biddle, "there is everything you could imagine here. Look! What about a doughnut? What about a cream horn? Or you could have a chocolate muffin, or a jam slice, or a coconut swirl."

"No," said Anna-Maria. "That's not what I want."

Mrs Biddle tried again.

"A coffee kiss? A currant bun? A cinnamon plait?"

"No," said the little girl.

"What about a slice from one

of these beautiful *big* cakes? There's a lemon sponge. Or look, a cherry loaf. A chocolate-chip log? A carrot cake? A double-decker date and walnut wonder?"

But Anna-Marie frowned again and shuffled her shoes.

"I don't like anything here," she muttered sullenly.

Mrs Biddle had plenty of patience. She needed it all now.

"Well, what *do* you like?" she asked. "The baker may well have some other cakes at the back, where we can't see them."

"Yes, that's true," smiled the baker. "What would the little lady really like?"

Mrs Biddle had told the baker about Anna-Maria's mother, so he too wanted to be kind to the little girl.

And Anna-Maria did know just what she wanted.

"I'd like a gingerbread man, please," she said, quite politely.

The busy baker's chubby cheeks looked a little pink.

"I'm very sorry," he said. "I'm afraid I haven't made any of those for a long time. My new ginger-

bread teddy bears rather took over, you know. Wouldn't you like one of those?"

"No, thank you," said Anna-Maria. "It has to be a gingerbread man, please."

"Well, I haven't any now," said the smiling baker, "but I will make some tonight specially for you. They will be ready first thing in the morning."

For the first time, Anna-Maria smiled. "Oh, *thank* you!" she cried. "That will be lovely!"

What neither Mrs Biddle nor the baker knew was that the little girl's mother made her gingerbread men on special occasions. Anna-

Maria thought that perhaps she would not miss her mummy quite so much if she had a gingerbread man just like the ones she loved at home.

That night, the busy baker had to work even harder than usual, and perhaps that is why he didn't pay quite as much attention to what he was doing as he should have done.

The next morning, Mrs Biddle and her niece called at the shop only five minutes after it had opened for the day.

"Here you are, sweetheart," smiled the busy baker. "Six little gingerbread men, just for you."

Anna-Maria looked down at the little biscuits in their special box. They were lovely, but her face fell as she glanced at them.

"What's the matter, darling?" asked Mrs Biddle. "Is there something wrong?"

The little girl looked up with tears in her eyes.

"They haven't got any buttons!" she said.

"What? Let me look!" cried the baker, taking back the box. "Oh dear, oh dear, you are quite right. They really *should* have buttons, shouldn't they?"

"Currant buttons," said Anna-Maria firmly.

"Yes, yes, that's just what I was thinking," said the baker, looking a little embarrassed. "I'm so sorry. If you come back tomorrow, I'll make sure I have gingerbread men with buttons. I was thinking of three buttons. Would that be right?"

"That would be just right," said Anna-Maria, for her mother's special gingerbread men always had three currant buttons.

That night, the baker worked hard again. In fact, he was so busy making sure there were buttons on his biscuits that the bread was left to rise for too long and almost burst out of the oven.

Next morning, Anna-Maria and

her aunty were waiting outside the shop when the baker opened the door.

"I've got them right here," he smiled. "And I counted the buttons very carefully."

Anna-Maria's blue eyes were bright as she peered into the box. There was a little smile on her lips. But suddenly her eyes clouded and she almost looked ready to cry.

"Whatever is it now?" asked Mrs Biddle. "They look lovely to me, sweetheart."

"But they don't have red smiley mouths," said Anna-Maria.

It was perfectly true. The jolly gingerbread men had little currant eyes and little currant buttons, but in his concern to make sure there were exactly three buttons on each little man, the busy baker had completely forgotten about the red smiley mouths made from cherries.

"Oh dear," said the baker, "I'm not doing very well for you, am I, my dear? Let me have one last try. Come back tomorrow and I promise I'll have the smiliest gingerbread men you have ever seen. Will you do that?"

"All right," said Anna-Maria. She wanted those gingerbread men so very badly, but she couldn't bring herself to tell her aunty or the baker why.

The day had started badly for the baker, and it didn't improve when his regular customers started to complain about the bread he had allowed to rise for too long.

"It's just not up to your usual high standard," said the Mayor, brushing crumbs off his waistcoat. "What's the trouble? Anything I can help with?"

"No," cried the baker. "Just a silly problem last night. Nothing I can't deal with, I promise you. It won't happen again."

But that night, the baker was so tired that he could hardly tell *what* he was doing. The only thing he could think of was Anna-Maria's sad little face.

He finished his other baking as quickly as he could (and perhaps he didn't take quite as much care as usual), then cleared his table so that he could concentrate all his efforts on the gingerbread men. This time, they must be absolutely perfect.

Soon six little gingerbread men were sitting on a baking tray, ready to go into the oven. They had one smiley cherry mouth. They had two little currant eyes. They had three currant buttons in a row down their tummies. They were just right.

With a sigh of relief, the busy baker popped the little biscuits into the oven and sat down.

He was exhausted! Slowly, his eyelids began to droop. His head began to nod. In less than a minute, he fell fast asleep at his bakery table.

Meanwhile, in the oven, the gingerbread men turned a lovely golden brown. But the busy baker slept on. The gingerbread men began to look a little toasted around their toes. But the busy baker's eyes didn't open. The

buttons on the gingerbread men's tummies began to sizzle, until they turned into little black cinders. But the busy baker didn't stir. Soon the smell of burnt gingerbread filled the bakery, and it was joined by the smell of burnt bread and burnt cakes and burnt biscuits. As the smell drifted across the bakery and tickled the baker's nose, he *jumped* out of his chair with a mighty shout.

"My bread!" he cried, flinging open the oven door. "My cakes! My biscuits! My gingerbread men!"

Everything looked dreadful. The busy baker couldn't imagine that even the ducks on the village pond would want to peck at his burnt offerings.

In despair, the baker glanced at the clock. It was almost seven o'clock in the morning. There was no time to make anything now.

The baker felt bad about his bread and cakes and biscuits. He knew how disappointed all his customers would be. But most of all, he felt awful about the little girl who was pinning her hopes on six smiley gingerbread men.

Anna-Maria wasn't waiting when the busy baker opened his shop door that morning, although several other villagers were. They stared in disbelief as the baker pinned up a notice. Within minutes, news of the bakery disaster was all over the village.

No Bread   No Cakes   No Biscuits

TODAY

Normal service resumes tomorrow.

No one felt angry with the baker. They all knew how hard he worked. They just felt very worried. What if he became really ill? And all because he always tried to do his best for his customers? Before the morning was over, the Mayor had called an Extraordinary Meeting, and everyone in the village (except the baker himself, who was sitting sadly in his empty shop) was trying to think of an idea that would help to make sure the poor man never became so tired again.

Things began to improve for the baker in the afternoon. And what had started off as the worst day of his life, soon became the very best.

At two o'clock, a little face peeped round the shop door. The baker hardly recognised it, because it had the sunniest smile he had ever seen. It was Anna-Maria, and holding her hand was a lady smiling just as broadly. The baker knew at once that it must be the little girl's mother. Their smiles were so alike.

"This is my mummy," said Anna-Maria. "She is better now and has come to take me home. And she brought me a present. I thought you might like one, because I heard what happened last night."

The little girl held out a gingerbread man, made by her own dear mummy. It was rather wobbly looking, and its smile was crooked, but the baker could see that Anna-Maria thought it was the best gingerbread man in the world. And she was right.

Just then, a group of villagers arrived at the door.

"We've come to help," they said. "You need some assistants, and we are going to take turns. We can start at once."

"Hurray!" the baker mumbled ... with his mouth full!

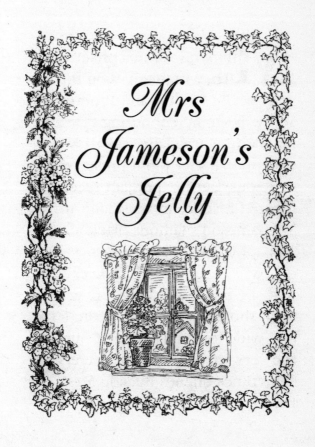

Mrs Jameson's Jelly

MRS JANICE JAMESON was famous for her preserves. They regularly won top prize at the Poultry and Produce Show in the neighbouring town. Her mandarin marmalade was truly exceptional. Her plum preserve was delicious. Her juniper jam received five red rosettes in a row. But it was Mrs Jameson's famous blackberry and apple jelly that really overwhelmed her public. Every jar that she made was fought over in the local shop. Visitors came from far and wide for the chance of buying the very smallest jar, and there were sometimes queues outside Mrs Jameson's house when the telltale

smell of simmering fruit wafted out of her windows.

Now Mrs Jameson was quite rightly proud of her jam-making achievements, and she enjoyed the praise of her friends and neighbours, but eventually their appreciation went to head — with rather disastrous consequences.

One day, Mrs Jameson was asked to give a lecture on preserving to the local branch of the Ladies' Luncheon Club. It was quite an honour to be asked, and Mrs Jameson felt a flutter of nervousness as she stood up to give her speech. But she need not have worried. As soon as she embarked upon her favourite subject, her anxiety left her.

Mrs Jameson gave her spellbound audience the benefit of her expertise on Selecting Fruits, Choosing a Preserving Pan, The Art of Stirring, Pots and Their Problems, Sinking Fruit: the Sloppy Simmerer's Curse, and Lovely Labelling. She held her listeners' attention so thoroughly that she began to feel as though no problem of preserving was so great she could not solve it.

"Now I will answer questions," she said grandly. "Who would like to begin?"

One or two ladies timidly put up their hands and voiced their own little difficulties. Mrs Janice Jameson dealt with these in brisk terms. She told one lady that her fruit was substandard and advised another to give up jam-making altogether, as she clearly had not the first idea about it. Other questions were dealt with in an equally robust way, and Mrs Jameson's audience began to be a little restless. Finally, a very superior-looking lady in an enormous hat gave a little laugh.

"It's delightful to know that such quaint old-fashioned hobbies are still being practised," she said. "Of course, those of us that have important work to do simply cannot find the time for such charming pursuits — even if we wanted to."

There was something in her tone that immediately annoyed Mrs Jameson. She felt that she did work as important as any you could mention. How dare the woman in the hat use such a patronising tone?

"I'm quite sure," she replied, "that any lady who is doing truly important work will have the intelligence and diligence to organise her time in such a way that she can pursue any hobby."

"But everyone has their limits, Mrs Jameson," persisted the lady in the hat in a silky voice.

"Nonsense," cried the speaker. "Such talk is for the fainthearted. Why, despite my numerous speaking engagements, I find time to make any amount of blackberry and apple jelly each and every year."

"Any amount?" queried the lady in the hat.

"Any amount," confirmed Mrs Jameson, who recognised a challenge when she heard one.

"In that case," continued her interrogator, "would you be willing to undertake to fill any empty jars that are brought to you? We would pay for your perfect preserves, of course."

"Certainly," said Mrs Jameson.

She thought quickly. Every year
when she came to make her jelly
there was a shortage of jars. This year
was likely to be no exception. It
simply was not possible that local
people could find so many jars that
Mrs Jameson could not fill them.

Mrs Jameson smiled sweetly at
the lady in the hat. "Perhaps you
would like to come and watch," she

said. "I'm sure you have a great deal to learn."

Oh dear, Mrs Jameson had made an enemy, and that is never a wise thing to do if you can help it. But she was very confident of her abilities. Making jelly came as naturally to Janice Jameson as sitting in front of the television does to most people. She could not wait to roll up her sleeves and go to work.

The next morning, when Mrs Jameson opened her front door, she found a cardboard box with thirty-two empty jars inside. She laughed scornfully.

"I can make thirty-two jars of jelly before breakfast," she cried, not entirely accurately.

Ten minutes later, Mrs Jameson was on the telephone to her favourite niece.

"Leonora!" she trilled. "Your services are needed. Please go out this morning and pick as many blackberries as you can find. I shall pay my usual rates."

"No problem, Aunty," said Leonora, who had heard from a

friend's mother about the Great Jelly Challenge and felt sure that her money box would gain from it.

That morning, Leonora went out and picked ten whole baskets of blackberries. She knew where the juiciest berries were to be found and was careful not to scratch her hands as she picked.

Back at home, Mrs Jameson sent her husband out to pick apples from the orchard.

"Only the best ones," she warned him.

"Yes, dear," said Mr Jameson, who had endured various tasks connected to his wife's hobby over the years.

By midday, Mrs Jameson had everything she needed. It was time to begin.

For the next few hours, the kitchen was full of delicious bubbling sounds. Mrs Jameson washed and peeled. She cored and chopped, and simmered and stirred. Finally, the moment of truth arrived. Mrs Jameson put a spoonful of jelly on a cold saucer and waited to see if it would set.

"Perfect!" cried Mrs Jameson, and she set about straining her jelly into jars.

By teatime, thirty-two jars of blackberry and apple jelly were standing on the kitchen table.

Thirty-two lids had been sealed, and thirty-two labels had been written (in Mr Jameson's best handwriting). Mrs Jameson felt tired but triumphant.

But next morning, when she opened her front door, she found another cardboard box of empty jars. This time there were sixty-four of them!

Mrs Jameson felt a little faint, but she was not going to give up. Summoning her troops (otherwise known as Leonora and Mr Jameson), she set to work once more. And by the end of the day, all sixty-four jars were filled, lidded and labelled.

There was no room on the

kitchen table for the new batch of
jam, so Mrs Jameson carefully
stacked the jars back in the cardboard box they had come in. Then
she wrote "This way up" in big black
letters on the box to prevent a sticky
accident.

You can guess what happened
the next morning. Over a hundred
jars stood on Mrs Jameson's
doorstep. She rose to the challenge,
of course, but I have to say that she
did not set about jelly-making that
day with her usual enthusiasm. In
fact, the troops were a little jaded as
well.

"I've picked all the best
berries," Leonora complained.

"Then you'll have to go farther afield," said her aunt. "I can't have substandard berries in my jelly."

Mr Jameson protested too. "My writing hand is aching," he said. "I think I may have done it a permanent injury."

"How do you think my wrists

feel," demanded his wife, "with all
that stirring and straining? Yes,
straining is the word, I can tell you.
The honour of our household is at
stake. We must go on!" she finished
dramatically.

Mr Jameson climbed reluc-
tantly into the apple trees again.
There were very few fruits left that
were worth picking.

Mrs Jameson put on a clean
apron and got to work. It was very
late when she finished, but every jar
was filled with jelly, and it is a
tribute to the tired cook's high
standards that the first jar tasted just
as good as the last.

Mrs Jameson went to bed,

confident that there could be no more spare jars in the whole area. It simply was not possible. Still, the next morning she opened the front door very gingerly.

It was a nightmare. There must have been at least five hundred jars standing on the step. Mrs Jameson had to sit down at the bottom of the stairs. In her heart of hearts, she knew that she could not fill five hundred jars, but she telephoned her niece all the same.

"No," said Leonora. "No, no, a thousand times no!"

"Double rates?" pleaded her aunt desperately.

"No!"

"Triple?"

"No!" And Leonora rather rudely put the phone down.

Mr Jameson's reaction was much the same.

"I'm only human, dear," he said. "I can't make apples appear on the trees. You've done your best. After all, you're only human too."

How Mrs Janice Jameson regretted her boastful words to the Ladies' Luncheon Club. How she wished she had known, as a friend helpfully told her at least three days too late, that the lady in the hat owned the biggest jam-jar factory in the entire country. Mrs Jameson felt that she never wanted to see another jam jar in her life.

At least the local shop had plentiful supplies of blackberry and apple jelly that year, but it was the last time it was to appear on the shelves. For Mrs Janice Jameson has sold her saucepans and taken up … knitting!

The
Woodman's
Daughter

ONCE UPON A TIME, there lived a hardworking woodman. All day he was busy in the forest, trimming and felling trees. Once a week, he would load up his cart with wood and set off for the nearest town to sell it. It was a long and tiring journey, and the woodman rarely arrived home before darkness had fallen.

When the woodman was very young, he met a pretty girl on one of his trips to the town. She thought him strong and handsome, and he was bowled over by her loveliness. For a whole year, they met once a week, and both began to long for the days to pass until their next precious meeting.

At last, the woodman plucked up the courage to ask the girl to marry him. To his delight, she agreed, and her father was only too delighted to welcome the hardworking young man into his large family.

"It is a pity you have no brothers!" he joked, looking at his eight remaining daughters.

The wedding was a simple affair, for neither the woodman nor his father-in-law had much money, but you have never seen a happier couple than the pair who left the church together.

If only it had lasted! At first all went well. The newly married couple were only unhappy when they were parted. But the wife began to realise that she must be on her own all day in the lonely forest. She was used to the town, where she could visit her friends or look in shop windows when she was bored. Here there was nothing but trees. The young wife soon began to feel that she hated trees more than anything else on earth.

The woodman could not understand why his wife became sad and silent. He had been brought up to a life in the forest. Nothing was more beautiful to him than an oak tree standing proudly in a glade, its branches outspread to shelter the little creatures who made their homes around it.

However, the young man understood that his wife might miss her family and her old home, so he took her with him each week when he carted his logs into town. The young woman came to long for those days, just as she had longed for them before her marriage.

Then, one day, the woodman's wife told him that she was going to have a child. The woodman was overjoyed. Not only did he long for a son to teach the ways of the woods, but he felt that his wife would be happier with someone to look after all day.

But as the time for the baby's birth drew near, the mother-to-be became more and more quiet and sullen. The woodman felt sure that it was simply that she was tired and longing for her baby to be born.

That week, when the couple went into the nearby town, everything was as usual. The woodman took his wife to her parents' house, while he went to sell his wood.

However, when he returned to collect his wife, he found her father at the door, looking worried and upset.

"I'm sorry, my son," said the old man, "but she refuses to return with you. She insists that she must stay here until the baby is born. Perhaps she is right. A woman should have other women about her at such a time. She will feel differently when it is all over."

The woodman was surprised and unhappy, but he could under-stand how his young wife might be feeling, so he kissed her gently and left her in the town.

Each week after that, the woodman rushed eagerly to his father-in-law's house to see his wife. And the third time he visited, he was greeted by the wonderful sound of a baby's cry.

The woodman flew upstairs to see his son. His wife was sitting up

in bed, the baby beside her in a
cradle. The young man hugged and
kissed his wife and asked how she
was. Then he turned to the cradle
and looked down on the most
perfect little baby he had ever seen.

"He's beautiful," he breathed,
touching one tiny hand. "What shall
we call him?"

"I have named her Agnes," said
his wife, hardly looking at the child
beside her.

The woodman was shocked.
"I don't know why, but I was
expecting a boy!" he cried. "Well, she
is lovely too, of course. And perhaps
we shall have a son next time, my
dear."

But his wife turned her face away and gazed out of the window with a faraway look.

The woodman could hardly wait to take his family home again. Each week, before he set out for the town, he put flowers in all the rooms and laid the table for two.

But each week, he returned alone to the forest. At first, his wife said that she was tired and unwell from the birth. The woodman was sympathetic and told her to stay as long as she liked with her family.

Later, when his wife was up and about, she said that the baby was too delicate for the long journey. The woodman had no experience of babies. His daughter looked strong and healthy, but he could not be sure. Perhaps it was right that she should stay.

Gradually, weeks turned into months. Soon, it was almost a year since the woodman's wife had come back to live with her family. The young man began to understand in his heart that she would never

return to live with him. His little
daughter would grow up outside the
forest.

Each week, the woodman went
to see his little girl. She seemed to
wait eagerly for his visits, and put up
her chubby little arms to be hugged.

Now it was the woodman who looked forward to his trips to town once again. They were the highlight of his week.

Then, one day, when the woodman called at his father-in-law's house, the old man met him at the door with a look of shame on his kindly face.

"My daughter is not here," he said. "She left this note for us. It seems that she met a soldier in the town and has gone overseas with him. She slipped out one night. We did not see her go."

The woodman felt as if a knife had stabbed into his heart.

"And my little one?" he gasped.

"Oh, she is here," said the old man. "She will be so happy to see her daddy again."

The woodman ran into the house and scooped up his little daughter in his arms. The tears ran down his weatherbeaten cheeks as he thought how nearly he had lost her.

"I am taking her with me," he said. "She shall live in the forest."

The fond grandfather tried to persuade the woodman not to take the little girl, but his mind was made up.

"I will bring her to see you every week," he promised.

So the little girl went to live

with her father. Every day, he took her with him into the forest, which she grew to love as dearly as her father did.

The years passed, and the little girl grew up. She was the loveliest child you have ever seen. And as time went on, she became a very beautiful young woman indeed.

Now it was the young men of the town who looked forward to the woodman's weekly visit, for his lovely daughter accompanied him. It was not long before she met a young tailor, and found that she liked him very much.

When the tailor shyly approached the woodman to ask for his

daughter's hand, he was not ready for the reception he received. The normally gentle woodman threw him across the street and warned him never to come near his daughter again.

"I cannot bear to lose you," he told his daughter. "And besides, marriages between townsfolk and forestfolk never work out. You must stay at home in future."

Now the woodman did not mean to be unkind, but he was afraid, so afraid, that the girl who had become the centre of his life would be lost to him for ever. In his fear, he could not think or feel properly, and so he made his daughter a prisoner in her home.

But the young girl loved her tailor, and although she loved her father too, she felt a new life calling to her. One day, when her father was at work, she packed her bags and walked the long miles into the town. She and the tailor were married that very day.

When he discovered that his daughter was gone, the woodman was beside himself with grief. He felt that he had lost the only thing in the world that mattered to him.

For the first time in his life, he did not go out into the forest, but lay on his bed and stared blankly at the ceiling. He foresaw day after day of dark loneliness stretching out ahead. It was too much to bear.

But as tears stained his pillow, the woodman heard the sound of a horse and cart growing nearer.

It was the woodman's daughter and her new husband.

When he saw his daughter's

happy face, the woodman could not feel angry or sad any more.

"Forgive me," he cried. "I thought I only wanted you to be happy, but I was really only thinking of myself."

"No, no," said the girl, putting her arms around him. "I know that you were worried for me and wanted to keep me safe at home. But my husband is a good man. He will bring me to see you as often as I like, and you shall come to visit us too. We have a beautiful little house, not quite in the town and not quite in the forest, but just where the trees end and the road begins.

Now the woodman cried tears

of joy. He understood that in order to keep something, you sometimes have to let it go free.

The woodman is old now. He no longer goes to the town with his logs, but he looks forward to his daughter's visits. They are the highlight of his week.

Besides, he now has a grandson who takes a great interest in the forest. The woodman is eager to teach the boy all he knows, which makes him very happy.

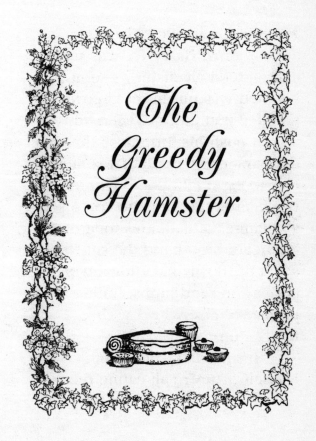

The Greedy Hamster

THERE WAS ONCE a hamster named Harry. He was a very greedy hamster. As soon as his food was put in his cage he gobbled it all up, and then he would push his little nose through the bars in the hope that something else to eat might come within reach. From his cage he could see all manner of delicious food on the kitchen table — and the smells! The scent of freshly baked bread was enough to send him spinning round in his exercise wheel with frustration.

"It's not fair!" he grumbled to himself. "They're all eating themselves silly out there and here am

I simply starving to death!" (At this point he would usually remember the large meal he had just eaten and that his tummy was indeed still rather full.)

"If only I could get out of this beastly cage, I could feast on all the food I deserve," he announced to himself, and the thought of all those tasty morsels made his mouth water.

One night after the family had gone to bed, Harry was having one last spin in his wheel before retiring to his sawdust mattress. As he spun around, he heard an unfamiliar squeaky noise.

"That's funny," thought Harry.

"The little girl oiled my wheel only today. It surely can't need oiling again." He stopped running and got off the wheel, but the squeak continued. Harry sat quite still on his haunches and listened intently. Then he realised it was the door to his cage squeaking. The door! The door was flapping open. The little girl had not closed it properly before she went to bed. Harry did a little dance of glee. Then he went to the door and looked cautiously out in case there was any danger. But all seemed to be well. The cat was asleep on a chair. The dog was sleeping soundly on the floor.

Now, as well as being a greedy

hamster, Harry was also clever.
Once outside the cage, the first
thing he did was look at the catch
to see how it worked. Yes! He was
pretty sure he could work out how
to open it from the inside now.
Harry sniffed the air. There were
some tasty titbits left over from a
birthday party on the table. He
could smell the sugar icing, and
soon he was on the table,

cramming his mouth with odds and ends of cheese sandwiches and pieces of chocolate cake. When he had eaten his fill, he stuffed his cheek pouches with ginger biscuits and ran back into his cage, closing the door behind him.

"Good!" thought Harry. "Now I will never be hungry again."

The next night Harry let himself out of his cage and helped himself to food, and again the next night and the night after that. He feasted on everything and anything — nuts, bananas, pieces of bread, left-over jelly and slices of pizza were all pushed into his greedy mouth. Each time he returned to his cage he filled his cheeks with more and more food. He did not notice that he was getting fatter and fatter, although he was aware that he could no longer run round in his wheel without falling off! Then one night, he undid the door catch but found he was simply too wide to get through the door!

For a while Harry sat in a very bad temper in the corner of the cage. His cheeks were still bulging with food from his last midnight feast, but the greedy hamster wanted more. Then he had an idea. "I'll get that lazy cat to help," he thought. He squealed at the top of his voice until the cat, who had been dreaming of rats, woke up with a start.

"What do you want?" she hissed at Harry. Harry explained his problem.

"Of course, I'd be only too pleased to help," said the crafty cat, thinking to herself here was an extra dinner! With her strong claws she bent back the door frame of

the cage, until there was just enough room for Harry to squeeze through. Then, with a mighty swipe of her paw, she caught him and gobbled him whole. She felt extremely full, what with Harry and all his food inside her. She could barely crawl back to her chair and soon she was fast asleep again and snoring loudly with her mouth open. Inside her tummy Harry, too, felt very uncomfortable. Every time the cat snored, it sounded like a

thunderstorm raging around his head.

"I must get out of here," he thought, and headed for the cat's open jaws. But he was far too fat to get out again. Then he had another idea. Through the cat's jaws he could see the dog lying on the floor.

"Help! Help!" he squeaked. The dog woke up to a very strange sight. There was the cat lying on the chair snoring, but she also seemed to be squeaking, "Help!" The dog put his head on one side. He was very perplexed. Then he saw a pair of beady eyes and some fine whiskers inside the cat's mouth. It was Harry!

"Get me out of here, please," pleaded Harry.

Now the dog did not very much like the cat, so he was quite willing to help the hamster.

"I'll stick my tail in the cat's mouth. Then you hang on while I pull you out," said the dog. "But mind you don't make a sound and wake the cat, or she'll surely bite my tail!"

The dog gingerly put the tip of his tail inside the cat's open jaws, just far enough for Harry's little paws to grab hold. Then he pulled with all his might. Out popped Harry and out of Harry popped all the food he'd stored in his cheeks

— peanuts, an apple core and a slice of jam tart!

"Thank you, thank you," gasped Harry as he made a dash for his cage and slammed the door shut. "I think I'll stay in my cage from now on and just stick to the food I'm given!"

Pumpkin Pie

Written by Angela Holroyd

IT WAS HALLOWEEN, and all the animals in Catsville County were looking forward to the annual Halloween Ball that was to be held that night. As usual, Tabitha Tatler had made the pumpkin pie for which she was justly famous, only this year she had excelled herself. This time she had baked the biggest pumpkin pie that anyone had ever seen. It looked so tasty that her neighbours couldn't wait to get their teeth into it, and it was so gigantic that it had to be stored in Tabitha's back yard, protected from the wind and rain by a tent.

That morning, just after the wintry sun had peeped out to say

hello, Tabitha bustled along to check
the pie. There had been a fierce
wind howling around the house the
night before and she wanted to
make sure that the pie was all right.
But Tabitha was in for a shock.
Instead of being perfectly round, the
pie had a large, gaping hole in one
side. And, what's more, it wasn't the
wind that had caused it, for all
around the hole there were teeth
marks. That could only mean one
thing — someone had been EATING
Tabitha's precious pumpkin pie!

Tabitha Tatler was most upset,
and before you could say "whiskers
and tails" she had spread the
dreadful news throughout Catsville.

The Mayor of the town was furious
— he always cut the first slice of pie
at the start of every Halloween Ball.
It was the grand opening to the
celebrations, and now someone had
actually had the nerve to bite a piece
out of it! All through the day everyone gossiped about who could have
done such a terrible thing — and the
name on most of their lips was
GREEDY GEORGE!

Now Greedy George was a very
large tabby cat with a big, fat tummy
and long, white whiskers. He lived
right next door to Tabitha Tatler, and
the thing he loved most in life was
food. He could eat more ice-cream in
one sitting than any other cat in the

county and, when he was hungry, you could hear his tummy rumble on the other side of town.

About 6 o'clock that evening, George was returning home from skating with his cousins in the country when he came face to face with a group of his neighbours. They were huddled together under a street lamp whispering excitedly. As soon as they saw George coming, they stopped talking and looked the other way.

"Hello!" called out George merrily as he skated up to them. But not one of them answered him. "What time are we all meeting tonight?" George tried again.

"*We* are all meeting at 8 o'clock," answered Perkins hotly. "But I shouldn't bother turning up if I were you."

"I'm surprised you've got the cheek to show your face, you greedy cat," added Tibby angrily.

George was baffled. He had not heard the news about the pie and was astonished when they told him — especially when they accused him of eating the missing piece.

"You needn't look so shocked," said Guss angrily. "After all it was you who pinched the last slice of my birthday cake."

"And my box of chocolate mice!" chipped in Ginger.

"And ever since Tabitha put that pie in the garden you've been drooling over the fence at it," said Max. "Why, only yesterday you said you'd do anything for a big, fat slice covered in cream!"

"But it wasn't me. I didn't steal any of it," George wailed.

But none of the other cats would believe him. After all, he was the greediest animal that they knew.

"And if you know what's good for you, you won't turn up at the Ball tonight!" said Perkins nastily. "You've already had your piece of pumpkin pie — and you won't be getting any more!" And with that they walked off, leaving poor George all alone in the windy street.

Now, George was not a bad cat. In fact, underneath his blustery, sometimes thoughtless ways, he was really quite kindhearted. Why, only the week before he had rescued a tiny mouse who had fallen in the river and had let him move into a hollow log at the bottom of his garden. But, although he was kind, George was greedy. There was nothing he liked better than a plate piled high with food, and everyone knew it!

"They don't want me to go to the Ball," blurted George to Marty Mouse the minute he arrived home.

"They think I stole the piece of pie. It's not fair."

Marty had already heard the rumours. To be truthful, it had even crossed his mind that George might be the culprit. But as he looked at his friend's miserable face, he knew that George was not to blame. He watched anxiously as George sat down heavily in his armchair. Then suddenly there was a loud rumbling noise. It was George's tummy rumbling! George was hungry! He looked up at Marty with a glint in his eye.

"If no one's going to believe that I didn't eat that bloomin' pie," snarled George, "then I might as well eat some of it!" And he rushed out of the door, pulling on his costume as he went.

Poor Marty didn't want to see George in even more trouble. But how could he stop him?

Once outside, George adjusted the wings of his costume. As a finishing touch, he tied a few red and yellow feathers onto the end of his tail. No one would ever recognize him now. He was dressed up as an enormous vulture — a big bird with a huge, sharp beak and fluffy collar.

"I'll show them!" whispered George as he crept along the fence that separated Tabitha's garden from his own. He had decided to creep up on the pie from the bottom of the yard, which backed on to a dense, dark wood. That way he was less likely to be seen.

No sooner had he entered the jungle of twisted branches and scratchy bushes, than the moon disappeared behind the inky clouds. But in the distance he could see a clearing and, in the middle of it, a huge tent — and there, inside the tent, was the biggest pumpkin pie George had ever seen. He licked his lips hungrily at the sight of it.

Not daring to look behind him, he edged his way to the side of the tent. It was quite dark inside except for the glimmering light from a large pumpkin lantern. George was just about to take his first bite from the pie when a ghostly voice behind him said,

"Stop what you are doing! I am the spirit of Halloween...!"

At the sound of the voice, George froze to the spot. He turned his head just as the voice rang out again. It was coming from the pumpkin lantern.

"I have come to give you a warning," it boomed. "I am here to tell you that you are making a terrible mistake. You did not take the first piece of pie, I know. But if you take the second, your friends will be

right to call you Greedy George.
Help me catch the real thief instead,
and you will be a hero!"

Poor George did not know what
to do. The pie looked so tasty, and his
tummy felt so empty — but he
didn't really like his friends thinking
he was a bad cat. So he moved a
little closer to the lantern and
stammered,

"Wh-wh-what do I have to do,
then?" But before the lantern could
answer, a scrabbling, scratching
sound came from a pile of leaves in
the corner of the tent.

"Quick! Hide!" urged the spooky
voice.

George did not need to be told

twice. He dived under the table in a flash. To his amazement, a mean-looking face with glittering eyes popped out of a hole hidden by the leaves. With a twitch of whiskers and a sly look around the tent, a big, brown weasel slunk into view. Standing up on his two back legs, the weasel sniffed the pie and licked his lips.

"Pumpkin pie!" he exclaimed and was just about the take a bite when George grabbed his legs and knocked him off balance. Before you could even say "Jack O'Lantern", the weasel was pinned to the ground. He struggled and snapped, but it was no good — George was much stronger.

Tabitha heard all the noise and came hurrying down the path.

"Here's your thief," said George gruffly, disguising his voice. "I just caught him trying to pinch a piece more pie."

"Well, bless my soul! If it's not Willy Weasel up to his old tricks again," said Tabatha. "I thought he'd

been booted out of Catsville County a long time ago."

"It's off to the kitchen with you," she said, taking the weasel by the ear. "I've lots of pots and pans you can wash up. Then we'll see what Sergeant Sam wants to do with you."

With that, Tabatha marched Willy Weasel off to the kitchen. But when she came back to thank the stranger in the vulture's costume, he had vanished — all that remained was one red and yellow feather, lying on the grass.

George slipped away, glad that Tabitha had not recognized him.

He was not sure that he deserved to be a hero. After all, if it hadn't been for the Halloween spirit, he would have been the one eating the pie. He had not liked the greedy look in Willy Weasel's eye one little bit. And he hated the thought of looking like that himself. Feeling miserable, he was about to slink off home, when Perkins, Guss, and Ginger appeared around the corner.

They had just been trick or treating and their goody bags were full to the brim with sweets and chocolates.

"Happy Halloween!" they cried when they saw George in his vulture's costume.

"Have a chocolate," said Guss, offering up his goody bag.

"Why, thank you!" said George in his gruffest voice, and then he did something very strange. Instead of popping the chocolate straight into his mouth as usual, he put it in his pocket and rushed off in the opposite direction.

"Who was that?" asked Ginger.

"Someone who wasn't very hungry," answered Guss.

"Well whoever it was, it doesn't matter now, because it's time we went off to the town hall to see the pie being cut," said Perkins, "even if Greedy George has been there first!"

Down at the town hall, hundreds of animals were streaming through the large wooden doors.

Everyone in Catsville County had arrived for one of the biggest parties of the year. There were brightly coloured costumes everywhere — witches, wizards, ghosts, and skeletons wherever you looked. The Mayor, dressed as a vampire, stood on a platform. Beside him stood Tabitha Tatler and in front of them was the pumpkin pie, complete with a gaping hole in its side. The Mayor began his speech.

"I would like to announce that tonight a mystery hero caught the Pumpkin Pie Thief, trying to steal a second piece of pie! It was none other than that rascal Willy Weasel, who is now in Sergeant Sam's care."

A loud murmur swept through the crowd as everyone began talking at once.

"Well fancy that!"

"I thought he'd been run out of town long ago."

"What a nerve that fellow has!"

The Mayor held up his hands for silence, then continued.

"We would dearly like to reward the hero, but he has disappeared. All we know is that he was dressed up as a vulture, and he left this behind." He held up the red and yellow feather.

Everyone in the hall turned to look at their neighbour. There were two animals wearing vulture costumes, but neither had the right colour tail feathers.

Perkins, Guss, and the others realized that they had seen the hero on their way to the town hall. They also realized how wrong they had been about George. They had been so sure that he was the thief and now they felt terribly guilty.

"I think we ought to go to George's house and say we are sorry," said Tibby.

"I agree," said Perkins who felt he had been the nastiest of them all. "And we could take our goody bags to share with him."

Meanwhile, George had gone home. He was disappointed at not

going to the Ball, but he was happy about something else. He had given his chocolate to Marty Mouse and it had made him feel much better about himself. George had discovered that thinking about others instead of always thinking about his tummy made him remarkably happy.

George told Marty all about the lantern voice.

"It was really spooky," exclaimed George. "I've never been talked to by a ghost before."

But instead of being impressed, Marty Mouse was laughing. Suddenly, he rolled up a piece of paper and boomed out, "I am the spirit of Halloween..."

"So it was you!" exclaimed George. "Why of all the..." but before he could finish, he burst out laughing too.

"My uncle told me who the real thief was," said Marty. "And I couldn't let you get in even more trouble yourself."

"I'm very glad you didn't," said George gratefully. "Come on let's have our own treats." But when he opened the larder door, it was bare. Then George remembered. He had made a complete pig of himself the night before and eaten every morsel.

"I'm so sorry Marty," he groaned. "It is true that I am greedy.

No wonder everyone blamed me for the stolen piece of pie!"

Just then there was a knock at the door and a voice called out, "Trick or treat!"

George opened the door with a heavy heart.

"I'm afraid that I don't have anything for you," he said sadly, staring at his feet.

"It's all right. It's us!" chorused his friends. There was a rustle of paper and they all lifted up a huge goody bag.

"We've come to say that we are sorry for what we said earlier, and to share our treats," said Tibby.

George invited them in and they

started to tell him about the mystery hero. Marty had to stifle a giggle, but George kept a straight face.

"The odd thing is," said Perkins, "that there were two vulture costumes at the Ball, but neither of them had..."

He was about to say "red and yellow feathers", when his eyes nearly popped out of his head. He had just caught sight of George's tail and tied to it were — red and yellow feathers! He had forgotten to take them off.

"It was you!" Perkins cried out at the top of his voice. All the others stared at George's tail as well.

"So you were the mystery hero,"

squealed Tibby excitedly, and she flung her paws around him. "Oh, George I'm so proud of you."

"It was... ahem!... nothing really," said George coughing and turning red. "I couldn't have done it without Marty."

"Nonsense!" snapped Marty. "I couldn't have captured Willy Weasel by myself. You were the real hero."

"You certainly were," said Ginger. "And now you must sit down and eat a hero's feast."

"Well, just a little perhaps," said George wistfully. "And I promise never to be greedy again," he said, passing the goody bag to Marty Mouse first!

The Christmas Kitten

Written by Andrew Charman

IT WAS CHRISTMAS EVE and everyone in the animal shelter was having fun. They were glad to be inside in the warm and not outside in the cold city streets, fighting over scraps of food. It was bright and noisy in the shelter and full to overflowing with cats of all shapes and sizes. Some were neatly groomed and others were shabby, but mostly they were cats from the streets who had nowhere else to go.

Ginger, the biggest and bossiest of the cats, had organized a game of tag. Cats were running and jumping everywhere. Suddenly, one cat pushed another as he ran past. The other cat pushed back, and a fight started. Soon others joined in. They fell into a heap, claws flashing, hissing, scratching, and biting. Like a hurricane, the fight swept across the room, gathering everyone in its path.

In the corner was a little kitten who was trying not to be noticed. The fight engulfed him. A paw struck him in the face. The kitten heard a buzzing noise and the room spun. Then suddenly he felt as if he was flying. He just had time to see the other cats below him looking up in wonder before he hit the ground with a bump. Ginger had pulled him out by his tail.

"You're going to have to keep

your wits about you if you're going
to survive in this place," laughed
Ginger. "What's your name, little one?"

"Oliver," replied the kitten,
trembling.

"It's a tough life in the shelter,
Oliver," said Ginger. "I can see that
I'm going to have to give you a few

tips on self-defence. Now, what do you do if a cat comes up behind you without warning?"

"Run?" suggested Oliver.

"No, you spin and slash," laughed Ginger. "Don't give them time to think." Ginger suddenly spun around and lashed out with his paws. His gleaming claws sank into the wall, leaving a row of deep scratches. "That's the way," he said, proudly.

"But I thought cats were supposed to live with families," said Oliver, surprised. "They sleep in front of the fire and lap up bowls of milk and have plenty of time for grooming."

"You're in the wrong place if that's what you want," laughed Ginger. "Around here we turn kittens into street-fighting tigers." And with that the big cat strolled off, muttering to himself.

Oliver washed his paw thoughtfully, and wondered at what Ginger had said. He had only been in the shelter for a couple of weeks and he couldn't remember very much about where he'd been before that. But he guessed he must have been with a "family," whatever that was, and that was how he knew about them. He certainly didn't like the idea of becoming a street-fighting tiger.

"Perhaps I am in the wrong place, then," thought Oliver to himself. Small and weak though he was, Oliver was strong in his mind. He knew what he wanted. He wanted to be in a family, and he was going to find one. He decided to escape.

Later, when the food arrived, Oliver saw his chance. As the others crowded around the bowls of food, he crept quietly out of the partly-opened door. He scampered quickly down the bright corridor and through another door. He was inside a cupboard. Then, just when he thought he'd have to go back and find another way out, he saw it.

A hole. What luck! It was just large enough for Oliver to squeeze through.

In no time at all, he was running along a narrow tunnel. He could feel a draught of cold air whistling through his whiskers. The outside couldn't be far.

Oliver heard voices ahead and suddenly the tunnel opened out into a large underground cave. He could see movement below him. As his eyes became accustomed to the dim light, Oliver saw hundreds of small, furry animals. They had sleek gray fur, long pink tails, and twitching whiskers. They were mice!

"Can we begin?" said a large mouse who had climbed onto an empty can in the centre of the throng. "I have called the family together to discuss an important issue." Oliver's ears pricked up at the sound of the word "family".

"Now as you all know," the big mouse went on, "tomorrow is Christmas Day and we have planned our

usual family celebration..." But he didn't get a chance to continue for Oliver could not hold himself back any longer. He jumped down from the ledge, shouting eagerly:

"Can I join your family? Oh, please let me join."

Chaos immediately broke out all around him. Mice fled in every direction. Oliver heard shouts of "Quick, cats!" and "Run for your whiskers!" as the mice climbed over each other to get away. Seconds later, the underground cave was empty. Poor Oliver couldn't understand it.

"Whatever did I say!" he thought to himself. "Anyway, that's

obviously not the right kind of
family for me." So he shrugged his
shoulders and walked on.

Soon Oliver reached the open
air. An icy wind was blowing
through the streets, and it had
started to snow. Large flakes fell
onto his fur and melted. Before
long he was wet and bedraggled.
The city looked strange and fright-

ening. Lights flashed and cars roared past. Oliver trudged along the sidewalk, feeling unhappier than he had ever felt.

Then Oliver heard an unfamiliar sound. He'd never heard it before, but he knew just what it was all the same.

"WOOF!" it went again. He turned and there it was, a little way

off, but getting closer — ears flapping, mouth dribbling, huge wet paws slapping against the ground. A dog! An enormous, hairy dog was bounding toward him.

One of the cats at the shelter had once told Oliver that dogs were harmless and that they just wanted to play. But Oliver wasn't about to stay and discover if that was true.

Oliver took one look at the dog's wet, wobbling mouth, and fled. For an instant, he was running on the spot, slipping on the icy ground. Then he shot forward, running as fast as he could.

Oliver rounded a corner and

glanced behind him. The dog was getting closer. Just then, a taxi stopped ahead of him. A woman who had been standing beside the road opened the door. Oliver didn't have time to think. He jumped straight into the open taxi and dived under a seat. The door slammed shut.

The dog skidded, spun around twice before stopping, and barked as he watched the taxi drive away through the snow. Oliver crouched under the seat and listened to his heart beating.

"Phew!" he thought. "That was close."

Oliver lay very still. Neither the driver nor the passenger had seen

him. They were busy talking about Christmas Day, just like the mice.

"I promised her one for Christmas," the woman was saying. "But all they had at the pet shop were rabbits and guinea pigs..."

No, they definitely hadn't seen him. The air in the taxi was warm and the vibration of the engine soothing. Soon Oliver was fast asleep.

He awoke just in time to see the woman opening the door. Out he jumped, scurrying quickly away into the bushes at the side of the road.

Oliver looked around him. He was on the edge of a wood. Tall trees stretched up toward the sun, their branches weighed down with the snow that had fallen only an hour before. It didn't look like the sort of place where you might find a family, but Oliver set off to search for one anyway. He struggled with difficulty through the thick snow. Sometimes he sank completely in drifts that came over his ears. Eventually, he came to a hillock which, for some reason wasn't covered with snow. He scrambled to the top to see where he was. Suddenly, the hillock moved. It rose from the ground, swayed slightly, and yawned.

The hillock wasn't a hillock at

all — it was a huge brown bear and Oliver was standing on it!

"I'm terribly sorry," said Oliver, nervously. "I thought you were a hill. I'll get down now and I won't bother you again."

"Oh, don't mind me," said the bear, yawning. "I didn't even notice you. I must have fallen asleep."

"Well, thank you," said Oliver

climbing down carefully. "Actually, I came out here to look for a family, but now I think I'm lost."

"Well, you're not lost now. I've found you," said the bear, kindly. "But I don't know where you'll find a family around here. You can come and meet my family if you like. We're just getting ready for Christmas."

Oliver said he would love to meet a bear family so the two animals walked on together through the sunshine. Soon they came to a big cave in the side of a hill.

"This is where we live," said the bear. "You're lucky to find us up. We usually sleep at this time of the year because of the cold."

Then the bear introduced Oliver to his mother and father and all his brothers and sisters, and they all sat down for something to eat. There were berries and grasses, funny-looking grubs, and bowls of honey, but no saucers of milk. Oliver decided that he wasn't very hungry.

After the meal, the bears rolled in the snow to clean their fur and started yawning noisily.

"Time for bed, I think," said the first bear. "Are you coming, little animal?"

But Oliver had decided that a bear family was not the right sort of family for him. It appeared that they did not have fires or bowls of milk, and he really didn't like the idea of rolling in the snow to get clean. So he thanked them for their kindness and told them politely that he would continue on his way.

The bears waved Oliver goodbye and he promised that he would return to visit them in the spring when they would all be feeling more lively.

The sun was hanging low in the sky as Oliver set off once more through the trees. Every now and then, a tree would shiver in the wind and send a cascade of flakes to the ground.

Everywhere Oliver looked he

could see footprints in the snow. Oliver tried to follow them, but he wasn't sure in which direction they were going. He went around in circles several times before reaching the other side of the woods.

Listening hard, Oliver could hear unfamiliar noises — animal noises that he had not heard before. He climbed a tall bank and peered cautiously over.

On the other side was the biggest animal Oliver had ever seen. It had huge sturdy legs that looked like tree trunks, large flapping ears, and an impossibly long nose. The strange animal was eating bundles of hay.

"Hello," said Oliver, bravely.

"And how are you this fine festive season?" said the animal in an important voice. "Would you like some supper? I have an apple here somewhere that I was saving for just such a visit."

The animal stepped back to rummage in the hay. There was a loud crunch.

"Oh, bother," said the animal, lifting its foot from the squashed apple.

"Actually, I wasn't looking for food," said Oliver. "I am looking for a family. Do you know where I can find one?"

"Well, we all belong to the same family really," replied the animal thoughtfully. "Each and every one of us belongs to the family of animals."

"Of course, we're not all the same," the animal continued. "Some of us are mammals, and others are reptiles or birds. Were you looking for any particular species? We've got most of them here. Take me for instance. I'm an Indian elephant. That's Mammalia, Proboscidea, *Elephas maximus*. What are you?"

"I'm a kitten," replied Oliver who was very confused and wished that he had a more important-sounding name.

"Come over here and let me have a closer look," said the elephant. "Yes, I see — four paws, fur, whiskers, long tail. Can you see in the dark?"

"Oh, yes," replied Oliver. "Very well!"

"In that case there can be no doubt about it," said the elephant. "You are a cat, a carnivore of the family Felidae. *Felis catus* to be precise. I would suggest that you continue your search for a family in the cat's enclosure. It's at the far end of the zoo."

Oliver thanked the elephant and hurried away. When he looked back at the huge animal, it was studying the squashed apple.

"Yes" Oliver heard the elephant say to itself. "Difficult things, flat apples. Now if I can just get my trunk underneath it, perhaps. . ."

Oliver scampered off through the zoo. He passed many strange and wonderful animals that he had never seen before. The chimps were throwing snowballs at each other. An owl winked a large, orange eye

at him. Snakes curled around
branches and flicked out their
tongues as he passed. A giraffe
peered down at him from a great
height. He never realised that there
were so many animal families to
choose from.

Eventually, Oliver arrived at the
cat's enclosure. He could hear a

fierce growling coming from inside. But he went bravely up to the fence and peeped in all the same. Inside was a huge cat with a long, sleek body striped with orange, white, and black.

"Excuse me," said Oliver.

The cat turned slowly and looked at him. Then it padded silently towards him and stared unblinkingly through the fence.

"I'm a cat," said Oliver, trying not to be put off by the other cat's menacing look. "And I'd like to join your family. Can I come and live with you?"

The huge cat looked at Oliver and slowly raised its eyebrows.

"Can you come and live with *ME?*" it repeated.

"Do you know *who I am?*" Oliver had to admit that he hadn't the faintest idea.

"I am a tiger," said the tiger. "I am the biggest and fiercest cat in the whole world. I am royalty, I am."

There was a pause while the tiger looked Oliver up and down again, and then he growled:

"SCRAM, PUSSYCAT!"

"So that's what a tiger looks like," thought Oliver, remembering his conversation with Ginger. "Well, I never wanted to be one of them anyway."

He went up to the next cage

and peered in nervously. Inside there was another huge cat, this time with a long, shaggy mane.

"Good evening," said Oliver politely. "Do you have a family I could join?" But to Oliver's dismay the big cat just laughed.

"Ha, ha, ha!" he snarled. "I am a lion, King of all the Cats. You're far too small and scrawny to be in my family." Poor Oliver! He backed away from the fence quickly and sat down heavily in the cold snow.

"Nobody wants me," he sobbed to himself. He covered his face with his paws and started to cry. He was so unhappy, he almost wished he was back in the animal shelter.

Suddenly a noise came from overhead.

"Psst!" it went. Oliver looked up. "Psst!" he heard again. Then he saw a scrawny cat beckoning to him from the top of a bank.

"Hey, Kitten," said the cat in a rasping voice. "You don't want to bother him, not if you know what's good for you. I heard what you said about looking for a family, and you're in the wrong place. Come with me."

The wise old cat led Oliver away from the zoo. Oliver could tell by the cat's accent that he came from the city.

"What you need, kid," said the

cat, "is a family of *HUMANS*." Oliver looked at him with surprise. "Don't worry," continued the cat whose name was Tom. "I know just the ones. I'll take you to them."

Tom knew all the tricks, and he led Oliver to a road with a row of houses. The two cats stopped outside a small house. It looked perfect. There was even a bottle of milk outside the door. The cat jumped nimbly up into a tree and walked along a branch that reached out toward the door. He pushed the bell.

There was a pause, then Oliver heard the sound of footsteps behind the door, and it swung open. A small, dark-haired girl looked out.

"Look Mum! Look Dad! It's a kitten. Oh, isn't he lovely?" The girl rushed forward and swept Oliver into her arms. "He's come to stay with us for Christmas. He's a Christmas kitten — just what I've always wanted" she cried.

"Well I never!" said her mother, and Oliver was most surprised to see the woman from the taxi. He looked around for the other cat, but he had vanished. The little girl carried Oliver inside and put him on a rug beside the fire, and her mum brought him a big bowl of milk.

"Oh, can we keep him?" asked the girl, excitedly. "You said this family needs a cat!"

"Well, yes, of course. If he wants to stay," replied her father. Oliver smiled to himself.

"Of course I want to stay," he purred. "I've got lots of grooming to catch up on."